Jungle Mischief

by David Regal
illustrated by the Thompson Bros.

Simon Spotlight/Nickelodeon
New York   London   Toronto   Sydney   Singapore

Discovery Facts

Pygmy Marmoset (PIG mee MAR moh set): A small member of the monkey family, found in the rain forests of South America. They eat things such as flowers and fruit, and even ants! They live high in the tangled branches of the jungle forest.

Three-Toed Sloth (slohth): A small mammal who also lives in South American forests. They are slow moving and very sleepy, dozing for up to eighteen hours a day! They are also strong. When three-toed sloths hang from a branch, there's no way to pull them off if they don't want to come off.

KLASKY CSUPO INC.

Based on the TV series *The Wild Thornberrys*® created by Klasky Csupo, Inc. as seen on Nickelodeon®

SIMON SPOTLIGHT
An imprint of Simon & Schuster Children's Publishing Division
1230 Avenue of the Americas, New York, New York 10020

First Edition   2 4 6 8 10 9 7 5 3 1   ISBN 0-689-83228-1

"Wow! I'm burning up!" Eliza said as the Thornberrys set up camp.

"We're in South America," Nigel explained, "just a stone's throw from the equator!"

"Cool!" exclaimed Eliza.

"No, *hot*!" chimed in Debbie. "Does this jungle have an AC control?"

Eliza rolled her eyes and said, "When you guys go out looking for things to film, I'm going to have a look around."

"C'mon, Darwin," said Eliza. "Let's meet some animals!"

"I'm dealing with one right now and his name is 'Donnie!'" Darwin replied.

Suddenly, they heard a scream!

"Don't move a muscle, you thief disguised as my sister!" shouted Debbie as she rushed out of the Commvee. "What did you do with my new tape?"

"I have *better* things to do than steal your tapes!" Eliza protested, "I can't believe you don't *trust* me. Let's go, Darwin. Oh, my binoculars! I almost forgot."

"Wait a second, I left my binoculars right here!" said Eliza. "Debbie, did you swipe them to get even for the tape that I didn't take in the first place?" Debbie mimicked Eliza as she replied, "I can't believe you don't *trust* me."

"I can't believe I'm related to you! Come on, Darwin and Donnie. Let's get out of here!" Eliza said as she stomped away.

"Who needs Debbie, anyhow?" Eliza said as they walked into the jungle.

"Not me!" answered Darwin.

"Me neither!" said a small voice.

Eliza, Darwin, and Donnie turned to see a pygmy marmoset smiling at them.

"Whoa! Who are you?" asked Eliza.

"My name is Click," answered the marmoset.

"What do you do all day?" Eliza asked.

"I like to have fun!" replied Click.

Click went up to Darwin, tugged on his tank top, and said, "You're the biggest marmoset I've ever seen."

Darwin smoothed his shirt and proudly told Click, "I'm *no* marmoset! I'm a chimpanzee!"

"You know," Eliza said, "you're just the kind of animal my folks want to film. How about following us back to camp?"

The minute they got back to camp, Debbie announced, "Now my hair gel is *gone*!" She saw Click and shouted, "Where'd that minimonkey come from? He's got my magazine! I bet he's the one who's been stealing my stuff!"

"He's been with me, Deb! He couldn't have done it!" Eliza pleaded.

"Why are you always defending these animals?" Debbie said as she entered the Commvee, slamming the door behind her.

"I don't understand what she said, but she sounded angry," muttered Click.

"Don't worry about *her*," Eliza said.

"Humans. They're like that sometimes," added Darwin.

"I think I've gone an hour without eating," complained Darwin.
"Do you have any snacks?"

Eliza opened her backpack. "Hey, my munchies are missing!"

"It wasn't me!" Debbie yelled. "But I *don't* like the look of your new
furry friend!"

"I'm telling you, he's a nice marmoset!" Eliza insisted.

"What is it with you and monkeys, anyhow?" Debbie asked.

Debbie muttered to herself. "Hmmm. I could rig up a big net . . . no, that wouldn't work. I could cover the ground with sticky stuff . . . no, too messy. I know, I'll set up a trap and videotape whoever's taking my stuff!"

"I have the perfect bait," Debbie chuckled as she set her blow-dryer out in the open on a table. "My Mega Blow 2000 is enough to tempt *any* criminal," she said as she tiptoed away.

"You're back already?" Eliza called as Nigel and Marianne returned from filming.

"Yes, poppet! We've caught the three-toed sloth on film, and it indeed has three toes!" Nigel exclaimed.

"There's a shock," added Marianne.

"Not only that," Nigel continued, "They spend most of their time hanging upside down, and often live their entire life in the same tree!"

"Doesn't that get boring?" Eliza wondered.

"At least they're not stuck in a Commvee," Debbie offered.

"I think it's time for me to check on my trap!" Debbie announced.

"What *trap*? What are you *talking* about?" Eliza asked as she followed her sister.

Debbie went back to the table where she'd left her blow-dryer.

"Oh man, it's gone already!" she exclaimed. Then looking at her camera she added, "But I've got you this time!"

"There's a thief around here and I'm going to catch him because I have a hidden camera!" Debbie announced.

"What would a *thief* be doing in the middle of the jungle?" Nigel asked.

"I can't believe you set up a camera, Deb, but at least *now* you'll see it wasn't me or my new friend who took your stuff!" Eliza exclaimed.

"We'll see about that. Come on!" cried Debbie as she led them all into the Commvee. "The camera was pointed right at the table. Whoever took my Mega Blow 2000 is caught on tape!" she explained.

"So let's watch it!" Eliza eagerly said.

"See? I *told* you that tiny monkey was behind all this!" Debbie triumphantly shouted.

Eliza stammered, "I can't believe it! He was *with me* most of the time."

"Video doesn't lie, lame brain!" Debbie insisted.

"I've got to find Click," said Eliza as she hurried off.

"I promise you, it wasn't me," Click insisted.

"I believe you," said Eliza, "but that still doesn't explain what I saw."

She took Click by the hand and led him back toward camp. "I'm going to clear your name," she told him.

"Don't ask me how I know, but I'm totally sure this little marmoset *didn't* take our stuff," Eliza explained to Debbie.

"Yeah, *right*," answered Debbie.

Marianne said, "I'm sure there's another explanation . . . but goodness knows what that would be."

Suddenly, Donnie started screaming and jumping up and down.

"He's trying to tell us something!" Eliza said, "Don't you see?"

"In what language?" asked Debbie.

"He wants us to go into the jungle!" answered Eliza.

"You know, I've never seen him quite this wound-up . . . today," Nigel remarked as they all followed Donnie.

Soon they came to a stop.

"Hold it. Am I seeing double?" Debbie asked, amazed.

"I can't believe my eyes!" shouted Eliza. "Another Click! But if my marmoset's over *there* . . . then who is *that*?"

Nigel exclaimed, "Of course! It's a known fact that most marmosets are born twins, and it looks like that one's a rather spunky fellow!"

Debbie complained, "He's no 'fellow,' he's a master criminal!"

"Aw, come on," said Eliza, "the little guy was just having fun."

"Why can't he just eat a banana, like a *regular* monkey?" Debbie grumbled.

"I knew you didn't do it," Eliza whispered to Click, when no one was watching.

"That's my brother Flick," Click replied. "He's always the nosy one who gets in trouble."

Eliza smiled and said, "Well, he can still be my friend. I'm very curious as well, and getting in trouble is something *I'm* pretty good at, too!"